They Brought The Change

Sara Saxena

ISBN 978-93-5610-439-6
© Sara Saxena 2022
Published in India 2022 by Pencil

A brand of

One Point Six Technologies Pvt. Ltd.
123, Building J2, Shram Seva Premises,
Wadala Truck Terminal, Wadala (E)
Mumbai 400037, Maharashtra, INDIA
E connect@thepencilapp.com
W www.thepencilapp.com

All rights reserved worldwide

No part of this publication may be reproduced, stored in or introduced into a retrieval system, or transmitted, in any form, or by any means (electronic, mechanical, photocopying, recording or otherwise), without the prior written permission of the Publisher. Any person who commits an unauthorized act in relation to this publication can be liable to criminal prosecution and civil claims for damages.

DISCLAIMER: *This is a work of fiction. Names, characters, places, events and incidents are the products of the author's imagination. The opinions expressed in this book do not seek to reflect the views of the Publisher.*

Author biography

Sara Saxena is a thirteen-year-old from India. She has had a passion for writing, and it has developed significantly over the past few years. She is intrigued by the Fiction and Fantasy genres. Her accomplishments on this planet over the past decade are many. But she can proudly say that the publication of her first book, 'They Brought The Change', was the happiest moment of her life. She has won multiple laurels in Academics at the District, State, and National Levels. She is fond of writing, reading, singing, and composing songs. She is a beautiful soul, a person everyone can turn to in times of need.

CONTENTS

Acknowledgements

I express sincere gratitude to:

My mom, Sanghamitra Saxena: Thank you for being my best friend, guide, and mentor.

My dad, Amit Saxena: Thank you for motivating me to be a better person.

This book is dedicated to:

All those who go the extra mile to bring about a change and transform lives.

The War That Ceased

Chapter 1 - The Proclamation of the Feared

"How durst you commit such a heinous crime, and have the valiance to stand in front of the savior of those you have wronged?" The King of Swimdom growled.

"I have wronged no soul. I have just repaid you," the King of Flyrille roared back.

The tete-a-tete between the two kings ceased with a declaration of war between both states. The Kingdom of Swimdom was responsible for releasing a surfeit of hazardous pollutants into the atmosphere above Flyrille. In retaliation, the King of Flyrille targeted one of Swimdom's most crucial resources, water, infecting it with all kinds of material they could gather. Ever since the proclamation of war, residents of both the villages have been anxious.

Ahim, a boy of fourteen, was particularly tense about this and had a strong opinion. "What good will war result in? The kings, just to fulfill their wraths, have heralded a war, which will lead to the complete annihilation of us poor villagers."

Adela, Ahim's sister, replied, "But the Swimdom residents did commit a grave mistake. Do you know how many people died due to high pollution levels? We cannot even relish soaring in the air without having to cover our mouths and noses! Remember, we are from Flyrille and will always be."

Saying this, she bent her knees, brought her hands forward into the air, and took off into the endless sky, which was earlier pretty clear and beautiful. Ahim got engrossed in deep thought watching his sister fly in the sky, along with other Flyrille residents. Few members carried groceries home, while some commuted to their workplace. But the sight was unpleasant as each one had to mask the mouth and nose to be safe. Ahim wrapped a cloth around his face and lifted off into the endless sky. After a few minutes of soaring through the clouds, he arrived in a cave-like place which he called 'Our Secret Den'.

"'Sidra, how are you? Did you hear the news about the war?"

"Yes, I did. And I am afraid we can't be friends anymore. My parents have strictly instructed me to break ties with all Flyrille residents I know," Sidra said with melancholy reflecting in her voice.

"That won't happen! We will do something. The war will never take place. Both villages will reconcile. But only if we take a step forward."

"I don't believe so, Ahim. And I expect you not to keep high hopes as well. What your kingdom has done is a sin in our religion."

Ahim frowned, knowing exactly what Sidra had to say about his kingdom's pathetic trick.

"Don't you know, we worship water? It is the greatest gift nature has given us. And your King, just to take his revenge, killed our sacred river?"

Ahim replied, "But you commenced it by contaminating our air. It is the only mode of travel we use. Our gift is the ability to fly and the clean air, which is no more clean, thanks to your kingdom!"

"But, water is not only our mode of transport but also our home! Our gift is being able to breathe underwater, which only we Swimdom residents can utilize. Now if there is no clean water left, where will we live and swim?"

Ahim was extremely ashamed of what both kingdoms had accomplished by playing these tricks.

"Sidra... Now is not the time to think of the past. We must think of a solution. I have an idea, but I cannot execute it alone under any circumstances."

Sidra was doubtful. Intending to cease an inevitable war? That seemed unattainable!

Ahim said innocently, "Come on. We have conquered tasks that the world thought were impossible. This would be a piece of cake for us, only if we join forces!"

"Ahim... Not everything is an adventure to be conquered. Sometimes you have to go with the flow of life. That is how it works. Let's stay calm and quiet and hope for the best." Saying this, Sidra slowly started taking baby steps into the forest, where they had acquired a shelter for their temporary stay, at least until the polluted river could be cleaned up.

As Sidra struggled to walk, tears flowed out of Ahim's eye. "I am sorry," he said.

"It's fine. Let's focus on the positive side. I am learning to walk like you, my friend, and that makes us a bit alike, right?"

Both of them burst out laughing. There was now some peace in the atmosphere. The tension reduced as the melodious chirping of birds was heard from a distance. The leaves of the tree started shedding off and fell to the ground. The next moment, both burst into tears.

Suddenly, Ahim started feeling a tinge of discomfort. He

coughed slightly. Sidra asked, "Are you okay?"

He assured her everything was fine. But the next moment he fell to the ground, holding both his hands near his neck, trying to breathe. He inhaled noisily. A certain terror stroke Sidra's face. She couldn't decipher what to do in such a situation. She tried to pick him up. "Nothing will happen! I am here! Do you know what problem you are facing? Where is your face mask?"

But Ahim's throat was so choked he couldn't utter a word.

Sidra succeeded in walking a few steps along with him. "I will take you to my cottage. Mother will have a cure. Don't worry!"

She had only walked halfway when her legs started aching badly. Her upper body too gave up. For someone who has lived in the water her entire life, coming up to the ground and straining the body was painful, and almost an impossible task.

Exhausted, she fell to the ground. Ahim was already unconscious.

Chapter 2 - Escape

When they woke up, they found themselves on an old torn carpet in Sidra's cottage. Sidra's mother was sitting beside her. "How are you feeling now, Sidra? I have applied the medicinal cream."

"Thank you, Mother. My limbs feel relieved. What on Earth had happened to Ahim? And how did you manage to treat him?"

Just then, Ahim's father walked into the room.

Ahim almost screamed, "Father? You are here?"

"Yes, my son. Now tell me why you stayed out in the air for so long! Don't you know the situation of the air quality here?" He yelled, looking furiously at Sidra's parents.

Just then, there was a knock on the door. It was one of Sidra's neighbors. She was a plump old lady with white strands of hair rising from her head. She said, "Can I get some-"

She stopped mid-sentence, as she was startled. Two Flyrille residents, in Swimdom? Especially after what they had done to the village? It was not acceptable to the villagers. Soon many young men gathered outside the house and started throwing stones at the cottage. "Traitors! Traitors!" They yelled at the top of their voices.

One of them rose, "They are surely conspiring against us with those Flyrilles."

Another one believed, "Yes, they might have been paid a huge amount to leak information!"

The door was locked now, but no one knew how long it could sustain. Ahim took deep breaths. Sidra patted his back to calm him down. His father was looking for options to escape. "Come, we can move out of this tiny window. No one will know."

They did so and reached their home. One could not say they had arrived safely. The cuts and bruises on their arms and legs narrated the entire story.

Ahim's Mother said to his Father, "Please do not scold him. He has to be explained in a proper way, not by raising the voice. That has never done any good."

As Ahim's Mother dressed his wounds, she cleared her throat sternly and started, "So... As you already know, we are on the verge of war with the Swimdoms."

Ahim said, "But Mother-"

"Hushh, we will speak today and you will have to listen. War, soldiers, barricades, regiments, conquest - these terms sound fancy and depict strength, power, wealth. Kings, within a fraction of a second, announce and cease wars. But do you know what is the unspoken rule of wars worldwide?"

Ahim replied, "That not the royalty, but the common man suffers the most."

His Father now said, "You are right. Have I ever told you, that you are more mature than most kids your age?"

"Umm- yes. You might have mentioned that, Father."

"Then, if we have a request, will you fulfill it?"

"Depends," Ahim said timidly. He was not sure how long his parents would refrain from losing their temper.

His mother could no longer control her emotions. "Please, stay away from Swimdom and its residents and the war! I beg you!"

"Mother, how can I do that? How can I leave my best friend alone in this time of need?"

His Father concluded, "You have no other option. You, Sidra, or anyone on this earth can do nothing to stop the war. You meeting her will only risk her life, as well as yours." Saying what he had to, he walked off into his room.

Ahim rested his head on his Mother's lap. His Mother caressed his hair and gently kissed his forehead. The silence of the night was broken by the distant barking of wolves, disturbed chirping of birds, and distorted noises of the neighborhood.

Those days, everything seemed devastated. Swimdom's water, Flyrille's air. Nature was deteriorating. The graph of environment quality decelerated with every passing day and humans could do nothing to stop this. From the residents to animals, plants, buildings, artifacts - soon everything would be affected by the poor air and water quality.

Ahim had accepted that their near future would consist of war, hatred, destruction, lack of clean air or water, food scarcity, famine, droughts, death - All for mere desire for revenge. Pondering over this, he fell asleep.

The next morning, he woke up to a piece of disastrous news. The Flyrille Village was on Red Alert, which meant that Flyrilles, till further notice could not step out of their house unless for extremely urgent situations. Ahim grimaced and walked away from the room, closing his ears with both his hands so he couldn't hear the villagers speak. The statistics of the number of deaths were disturbing to listen to. Around hundreds had been showing severe symptoms of respiratory illnesses and breathing problems; while a few others had surrendered and made their place in the afterlife.

Ahim discussed with Adela, "What about the war? Will it take place?"

"Isn't it pretty evident it will?" She answered back in a span of a few moments.

"But wouldn't that mean risking soldiers' life?"

She rolled her eyes around the room and then thought for a while. "Yes, it would be like forcing our soldiers to climb a steep tree just to bear the sweet fruit at the top."

Ahim said, "And in this case, the sweet fruit is both the kings' power and position. I wonder when they would let go of their ego and think about the masses for a change."

"And I wonder when you would stop worrying about things that are not under your control." Saying this Adela strode to the kitchen.

On the other hand, Sidra too heard the disastrous news. She sighed, her eyes weary and hair disheveled. She had been melancholy ever since the last meeting with Ahim, wondering what to do next. The situation in Swimdom was no less. Hundreds could not adapt to the new environment. They were so used to living in water, that coming onto land had disastrous effects on their body, also causing death ultimately.

While in the palaces, preparations for the war were in full swing. It was to be held on the seventh day of the last month of the lunar calendar. The soldiers were being trained harshly in both the kingdoms. But this could not continue, as numerous soldiers fell severely sick and thus became unfit to fight the war.

Both the kingdoms were rich and had a surplus of military strength. But, such kind of a situation never arose since the deadly virus had broken out a few decades ago. What would the kings do now? How would they commence a war with no soldiers?

Chapter 3 - The Worst Nightmare Comes True

Ahim hoped that the war be terminated and peace restore in both the villages. After all the riots and violence that had been taking place in the past few days, an announcement of the cancellation of the war would probably convince the citizens to opt for the non-violent way.

The King of Flyrille was to address the residents this evening. All residents of Flyrille, as well as those of Swimdom, waited with avidity in their minds. Exactly at half-past seven, everyone eagerly rushed out of their houses, leaving all work undone, just to hear what the King had to herald.

They halted at their doorsteps. One couldn't move forward, as the village was still under red alert. The messengers of the King came riding on their beautiful milk-white horses. They took out a piece of parchment paper, on which the royal message was written in bold. One of the messengers read out in a loud and deep voice, "The King calls for your service during these crucial times. As you know, the number of our military officials has decreased rapidly. Hence, all men loyal to this village are expected to join the army and fight the war from Flyrille's side."

Declaring this, they moved forward on their horses to other streets, where people waited to hear the termination of war instead of this awful piece of news. But, fate was not with the residents.

Ahim was boiling with rage. "How could the King do this to us? Sending the common men to the warfront and endangering their lives? And what about the Red Alert?"

Adela said, "Does that mean Father will have to join the war too?"

"Unfortunately, yes, Adela. The commanders will not let us live in peace if Father doesn't lend a hand."

Adela said, "They are so heartless. Now that Father would have to be a part of it, this war should never commence in the first place!"

Ahim replied, "You have realized this pretty late." He sighed, looking at his little sister whose eyes were glistening with tears. "Well, better late than never. I believed this was absolutely wrong from Day One itself. But no one paid heed to my words!"

"I am so sorry I opposed you, now I know what it feels like to be scared for the life of a loved one."

In the next room, Ahim's Mother was tense. She continually stroked the nape of her neck while taking heavy breaths, sprinting across the room. She finally said, "We're peasants! We don't know how to fight. We haven't held a weapon in our hands our entire lives! How could they expect you to serve in the Kingdom's army?"

Ahim's Father said, "It is completely unfair. But I have to go. Otherwise, they could harm you, Ahim, and Adela. I cannot bear to see that situation."

"But what if something happens to you? What if you don't return safe and sound? I cannot live to see that day."

"Whatever happens, remember, I will always find my way back to my family."

Ahim's Mother burst into tears. Ahim and Adela too walked into the room, their eyes swollen from crying.

Ahim said, "Father, we made this for you." He gently put a paper flower in his Father's hand. Ahim's Father narrowed his eyes and read, "Ahim and Adela's SUPERHERO!"

Ahim's Father said to them, "This is beautiful! I will preserve this for eternity. I will take it with me when I leave. What could possibly harm me if my children's well wishes are in my side pocket?"

All of them shared a family moment, something so special that it was engraved into their memories for the rest of their lives.

After a few days, it was time for Ahim's Father to leave for training. The situation of the masses was better with regard to health. The Red Alert had been removed, and people were once again free to roam around and fly in the sky as they please, but at one's own risk. Ahim's Father and other villagers were to gather in the Central Village and then move towards the Royal Palace together. There they would have a tiny room in the name of soldiers' quarters where all of them would stay. Ahim and Adela remained locked in their rooms, while Ahim's Mother saw his Father off. "So long," she said.

"So long," came the reply.

Meanwhile, Ahim and Adela were utterly upset. Adela was lying on the bed with her chin cupped in her hands, pretending to read her book. Ahim stood near the window, watching his Father fly out of the house right into an unpredictable pool of danger.

It was a few minutes after his father had left, Ahim's eyes fell over the paper flower that they had gifted, lying on the table. "Father must have forgotten to take this along with him!"

Chapter 4 - Mission Peace

Adela heard what Ahim had said and she too looked over. "But he said this flower would protect him!"

Ahim pondered, "Father would need this as a symbol of courage and hope; something which would remind him of us. I have to go and hand this to him before it is too late."

He rushed out of the house as if he wished to get on a running train. He flew and flew for miles, just following the path his nose led him to. This path was long and filled with fear and doubt. What if he had missed his Father? What if he could never see him again? All these thoughts crossed Ahim's mind and shook him from head to toe.

He reached Central Village, but it seemed like he had flown to the end of the world. Alas! The troop had already left for the Royal Palace.

Ahim sat down in the middle of the crowded place, crying his heart out, with his face buried in his hands which were placed on his knees. Many people walked by but didn't bother to ask. After a few moments, he gathered himself up. He held his head high and said, "I will not lose courage. I will be brave and go to the Royal Palace. I will only stop when I give this flower to my Father, in his own hands. I will make all efforts so that the war does not take place."

With the right reason, motivation and willpower, Ahim could achieve anything he desired. Now that he had acquired the right mix of all three, he set out on his quest to restore peace in both the villages.

He flew all night, battling the cold, predators, and negative thoughts. He received food and warm clothes from some nice accomodating individuals. He thanked the kind strangers who had helped him and continued his journey. The morning, along with it, brought rays of bright sunshine, the sight of the magnificent Royal Palace, and the hope that a boy of fourteen could make a difference.

When he entered, only a few strangers were walking and flying past him - his Father and other villagers were not in sight. He asked the first person he saw, "Where are the villagers that had arrived for training this morning?"

The person replied while signaling in the right direction, "There - in the Common Court."

"The Common Court?" Ahim looked baffled.

"The Kings of both the villages have gathered there for a meeting."

"Thank You," Ahim said hurriedly, and then rushed off to see his Father.

After a few moments, when he finally saw his villagers, he breathed a sigh of relief. They were training on the enormous ground, with all kinds of equipment that could harm the opposing kingdom's army.

Ahim ran and stood in the middle of all trainees. The Flyrille King was standing on a raised platform with his servants and bodyguards. The Swimdom King was also present there.

Ahim took a deep breath. He then yelled, "I want to say something! Please hear me out!"

Chapter 5 - The Valor of Children

Everyone turned their heads around to see the source of the voice. When they found Ahim there, they were lost in deep thought. Why had he come here, and what did he have to say? The King of Flyrille admired the little boy's courage and let him speak. The Swimdom King did not utter a word but eagerly waited to hear Ahim speak.

"Your Majesty, thank you for lending me your precious time and granting me an opportunity to speak. Today I want to appeal for the cancellation of the announced war."

The trainees were startled, and Ahim's Father begged him not to say a word. But Ahim couldn't refrain himself today.

"The Kingdom of Swimdom, due to their carelessness and irresponsible handling of hazardous material, have polluted our atmosphere which has caused us enough trouble. We have been through such a difficult phase the past few months. Almost every house was infected and fighting for their lives. We have also lost many lives. Our ability to move in the free air has been snatched."

"That is why the war has been decided upon! Those Swimdoms need to learn a lesson," The King said.

"We already did!" shouted the high-pitched voice of a young girl. It was Sidra. "Your Majesty! I am Sidra from Swimdom. Ahim is my friend, and he is absolutely right. I saw him flying anxiously and followed him here. If you permit, could I also say something?"

The King loved children and their innocence. He was

sensible enough to never harshly punish Ahim or Sidra, no matter what they said. Ahim knew about this, and thus he hoped to convince the King to rethink his decision. The King now said to Sidra, "I am curious to know what you want to put forward."

"Thank you! We were peacefully living in our habitats and homes created underwater. But our happy life was invaded by a plethora of chemicals? Earlier, our water was so clear one could see the civilization inside. But now, it has turned grey and green. All our homes and houses have been lost. The world underwater is now inhabitable. So many of our mates died in their houses when the first surge of pollutants entered. They could not survive. It was God's wish that we survived. But our life now is so much worse! Numerous people didn't adapt to these new conditions, as you already know. We have faced our hardships, and are finally trying to move back to our normal lives."

"Our aim of telling you these happenings was to make you aware of our situation," Ahim clarified.

"But that is why we have prepared to launch a war and get justice for all of you!" The King said.

Sidra boldly said, "Both the kingdoms have had their bad days due to these past mistakes. We have already had our share of challenges and hardships. If this war takes place, us villagers would have a much harder time than we have had in years."

Now was Ahim's chance to convince the King. He said, "I will tell you what we can expect of this war.

All men, fighting at the war front, with wives and children waiting anxiously at home, praying that they come home in one piece..."

Sidra continued, "Loads of destruction, damage, death in

the battlefield as well as the respective villages..."

Ahim added, "Shrieks of innocent people battling for their life, children crying, people yelling..."

"People who haven't committed a single wrongdoing in life suffering... "

"Children getting orphaned at a young age, women getting widowed..."

"We could continue forever. But do we want to?"

There was silence all over. That day was noted in golden in the pages of history, for it was the day when people were convinced that children sure are a gift of God, and their pure mind is what makes them precious. The Kings knew what war would bring, but they were too ignorant and scared to call off the war as it would tarnish their reputation. They just needed the push that Ahim and Sidra successfully provided.

After a few days, Ahim was talking to his fellow villagers and friends.

"It was quite a task, wasn't it?"

"It sure was."

"This surge of environment deterioration and diseases made me realize that there are so many facts that the authorities are hiding from the common man," Ahim said mysteriously.

"What?" The others asked.

Ahim replied, "The fact that Mother Earth is taking her revenge. It is not one factory's smoke emission or sewage disposal that led to this situation. The offensive and defensive measures taken by the kingdoms have just aggravated the already existing problems. This is not about Flyrille or Swimdom. It is much larger than all of us. It is about the environment, nature, our home planet Earth.

Did you know, that we are destroying it every single day?"
"Yes, it is because of our own deeds the ecological balance
has been disturbed," said one of his acquaintances.
"And to put the entire blame on the Kings would not be
right. This situation arose now because of them, but it
would have arisen in a few years anyway if not now."
They all finally agreed, "We will each contribute towards
saving the environment by doing our bit. After all, do we
want this situation again?"

The Stolen Horse

Chapter 1 - The Secret in the Stable

If one had to choose, from among all adolescents in the world, the one who is the most righteous of all, it would probably be Kay. And if one had to choose the complete opposite, it would be Aina. That was what the public image of the Parson Duo was.

Aina had executed several mischiefs, but Kay had saved the day every time. There had never been a severe issue with them.

But one day, an act of theirs got the better of them.

It was six in the morning. The rays of the morning sun shone onto Kay's eyes, bugging him a little. He opened his left eye; and reached out to the window to block the sunlight by moving the curtains. Just then, someone opened the window from the outside and quickly jumped in.

"Ah!" Kay shouted in shock.

"Shh!" She said.

"You, what are you doing here?" Kay asked.

"It's my house, and I can be anywhere I want to," came the reply.

"Who enters their own house through the window, like a thief? You're a little absurd sometimes," Kay said.

"Well, I am meant to be absurd... because I am your sister!" Aina giggled at the top of her voice in the most unpleasing manner.

"Unfortunately, yes," Kay said as if he was sick and tired of his little sister's boisterous behavior.

Aina suddenly got tense. "I wanted to tell you something. Come to the stable, and be quick." Saying this, she disappeared into the flight of stairs outside the room.

As Kay dressed up for the day, he wondered why Aina had called him to the stable. He knew she had a soft corner for animals, especially horses. But she also knew he loathed being around animals, for he was a germophobe. Why, then, did she want him near the stable?

Kay entered the stable covering his mouth and nose with a handkerchief. Aina was walking to and fro, breathing heavily and in deep thought. Kay pondered over the idea that his little sister might be in a grave crisis, for she had never been so tense. Just this morning, she looked fine. What had happened now?

Aina said, "Come here. I want to introduce you to him."

Kay said, "You know I can't come in. It's very unclean. Who's 'him'?"

Aina was pretty anxious and said, "Quick, he's here. I can't possibly handle this situation without you."

As Kay darted in, he said, "Please don't tell me you have committed another blunder. I had barely saved you the last time. You know we cannot indulge in such things."

Kay reached where Aina was standing. She pointed to a horse and said, "Look at him, so poor and vulnerable!"

Kay was startled and baffled, "That's it? You were so tense about a horse? I will tell the servants to feed-"

"No! I mean, we cannot tell anyone about him. He is not one of 'our' horses."

"What do you mean?"

"Umm... I... I might have gotten it here from someone else's stable."

"Oh, okay." Then, a realization struck him. "Wait, what? You stole it?"

Chapter 2 - Trouble for Kay

Aina froze at her place, her chin dipping down. Her spine was bent, and her head faced her shoes.

"Remember this morning when I said that you were a little absurd sometimes? Now I know. You are always very absurd," Kay said, expressing sheer disappointment.

"I am absurd, and I am sorry! But you must help me now," Aina said when she had ultimately summoned all her courage.

"You need my help to conceal a crime? Since you are old enough and can make major decisions like stealing and lying, you can also manage your own mess," Kay said, moving his hands in all directions.

"I am only thirteen and a half! So technically, I am still a child... I need your help," Aina whispered, loud enough so Kay could hear her.

Kay stood with crossed arms and narrowed eyes. He grimaced, then glanced away.

"We must think of something to stop the situation from getting out of our hands," Aina enunciated.

Kay said, pacing in short spans, "The situation is already out of our hands! We can't maintain this horse on our own. We can't inform anyone since that will only defame us of robbery." He was sweating excessively. Aina could hear his heartbeat rising by the moment as if it was planning to jump out of his body.

She asked, "Haven't you faced such situations in all your

nineteen years?"

"No, not at all! I didn't go around stealing other people's property," Kay shrieked.

Both of them were anxious, as one would react in such a situation. After all, it is not every day that a stolen horse rests in one's stable.

Kay suggested, "I will call Neil, and we will take care of it. We will return it to the owner."

"No, we can't do that!" Aina was scared out of her wits.

Kay remained silent. He didn't know how to handle his sister's tantrums.

He said, "Don't you think the owner will come looking for his horse? Who did you steal it from?"

She replied, with descent in her voice, "Umm... Mr. Devin..."

Kay raised his eyebrows in utter disbelief. "Mr. Devin? Neil's father?"

Aina rolled her eyes in every corner of the stable to avoid Kay's cold stares of surprise, annoyance, and bewilderment.

"What on earth made you do that? Neil is my best friend and my business partner! How will I face him now? Mr. Devin is our father's close friend. They will find out soon enough!"

Kay then recalled that they had visited Mr. Devin's house the day before. He asked, "Did you see the horse when we toured his barn yesterday?"

"Yes," she meekly replied.

"I knew I had seen him before! It's the horse I had expressed interest in while talking to Neil yesterday. Would he think I stole it? But why did you have to do this, Aina?"

"I can't tell you the exact reason. The first time my eyes

had rested on this impoverished horse, I knew I had to get him home. I sneaked in there at night and brought him along. Trust me on this."

"Trust?" He sighed. They had reached an impasse. Nothing could be explained to Aina anymore. She had lost her mind, Kay thought.

Chapter 3 - Dreading the Possibilities

After a few moments, they understood that the horse had to be fed. Aina figured out the food for the horse and was feeding him while Kay was busy deciding the next plan of action.

Kay said, "What do you think we should do now?"

She replied, "Maybe we should start with a name for him. How about Knight Rider?"

"That should work," Kay said in a disappointed tone, for his sister was still ignorant of the consequences. "I will ask you for the last time, why did you steal the horse?"

"I will tell you for the last time. I did it because I felt like doing so. And he needs us." Her eyes strayed past Kay.

"I don't believe you. There is no need for you to steal. We have so many horses. And Mother and Father have never taught us to rob. We come from such a reputed family. Tell me for real, what made you risk the family name for such a petty thing?"

Aina did not utter a word. She couldn't.

Kay had something in mind, but he hadn't expressed it. He had kept it buried in his heart for a long time. But now Aina was driving him up the wall. He had to say it, no matter what she thought.

"Isn't it suspicious? Stealing my best friend's horse?" Kay asked.

Aina had no answer.

Neil and Kay were indeed very close. It was a fact. No

external entity could alleviate their friendship. They had accomplished everything together - completing school and college, handling their fathers' joint business. Kay spent more time with Neil than with his little sister or family.

Kay considered the whole situation to be a complete mess; and that it would alter the way Neil and Mr. Devin felt about him. This time, his image and entire reputation were at stake due to his little sister's disastrous blunder.

"I have so much respect for Mr. Devin, and he adores me too! He knows how passionate I am about the project. That is why he has chosen me to assist Neil in running his business... After this incident, everything changes. Do you even have the slightest clue of the after-effects?"

Aina turned her head around and hid her face in her hair.

"You always make my life problematic, Aina."

Aina took a short breath and calculated what Kay had just said. She glimpsed at him with eyes wide open but then turned her head down and looked at her shoes. Her mind was somewhere else. Soon, her eyes filled with tears, and when she couldn't restrain herself anymore, she burst into a pool of tears.

She sobbed, "Do you consider me your enemy? You are not devoid of crimes either."

Chapter 4 - Kay's Mistakes

Kay paused. His body posture perked up, and he said in a curious voice, "What have I done?"

"When was the last time we had a conversation this long?"

"The... I... I don't remember. But that... that doesn't prove anything, does it?"

"And when was the last time you asked me how school was? Or if I was making any new friends?"

"It has been a long time, I agree."

"You have forgotten your sister under the guise of business and partnership with Neil."

Kay did not utter a word. He knew he had already passed harsh remarks, and his little sister need not endure more. He was at fault in this situation, but he could do nothing to make things better at the present. They decided that it was enough, as they had a bigger problem to cater to - the horse!

Kay finally said, in his mature tone, "We can't return it to Neil; he can't know it was us. We will sneak into his stable at night and drop off the horse."

"Knight Rider, that's his name now. And we cannot send him to that house at all. Trust me. Please."

"I don't trust you. If we can't send him back, you should think of a viable solution now."

"He will stay with us for a few days until we find someone worthy enough for him," Aina suggested. "Will you please help me take care of him?"

"Yeah, I guess. We will be in hot water if the elders find out. Weren't we clashing just a few minutes ago?"
"Well, yes, but that's how siblings are. We are quick to quarrel, and quicker to make amends."
"I can help you conceal him from the family, and I will back you up in difficult situations. But do not expect me to go near that horse."
"Knight Rider!" Aina yelled.
"Yeah, I know. But I don't know if he has had a bath recently. He might be full of germs, who knows?"
"See, I am touching him. He's clean, come on," Aina insisted.
"I better stay here," Kay smiled.
Aina was relieved seeing the slight smile on his face, for it said that Kay didn't mean what he said and that he was with her in the battle.
Kay said, "We cannot keep him in our stable. The workers will realize and report his presence to father."
Aina's glowing eyes indicated the occurrence of an idea in her mind.
"I know a place. This afternoon, when everyone's asleep, we will silently take him there," she instructed.
"We should get him out of sight before the workers come to feed the horses in the afternoon," Kay hoped.
"For now, we should get going. Mother might be looking for us," Aina said.
Aina and Kay met their Mother and went back to their rooms as if it was just one of the ordinary days and that they had not stolen a horse and held it in the stable. Just as virtuous students do, Aina tried to get engrossed in their books. Kay tried checking some paperwork. But neither of them could keep themselves from thinking about Knight

Rider. The thoughts of the stolen horse, that is, Knight Rider, as Aina had named him, kept lingering in their minds. They anxiously waited for lunch because after eating, they would be able to visit Knight Rider once again. They wouldn't be at peace till they transport him to a safer place.

Chapter 5 - Trip to the Hideout

It was afternoon. All the family members and workers were resting. Aina and Kay slowly slipped out of the house into the stable. Knight Rider was lying there. Aina went near him and caressed him.

"You should be careful around him," said Kay. "Animals are unpredictable.

But Aina was assured Knight Rider wouldn't do anything that could possibly harm her. When she realized that Kay hadn't looked at Knight Rider properly even for once because he was so bothered about being in the unhygienic place and repeatedly kept dusting off his clothes, she said, "Where are your eyes at? Look at this beauty here."

Kay turned his head to get a proper view of Knight Rider. His face lit up with radiance and his cheeks glowed. He smiled because it was indeed beautiful. From the outside, it looked like a victim of wear and tear. But there was something about him, maybe his inner beauty that attracted both Aina and Kay.

Then, his brows drew together and his expression changed noticeably. A beam of doubt had struck him. "Aina, you said this was Neil's horse. Then why does it look like this?"

Aina said, "Umm... like what?"

"Like it's overworked and undernourished? Mr. Devin, the richest person in town, definitely feeds his horses well, right?" Kay said.

Aina laughed awkwardly.

Both of them led Knight Rider outside the stable. The road was desolate; there was no living soul in sight. They did not fear being caught there. They walked for a few minutes without communication. Then Aina had the urge to say something she had buried in her mind for a long time. With tremendous courage, she commenced a conversation on the conflict they had had.

"You blurted out some cruel things in a fit of rage this morning," Aina said.

"You did deserve a little reprehension," Kay quickly reverted back.

Aina sobbed a little.

Kay said, "Aina, stealing is morally wrong. And I am not going to comfort you or tell you that it was okay to have done that, because it was not..."

Aina asked, "Do I... Do I trouble you a lot?"

"Well, you are a little notorious," Kay answered.

She had started out on the mission of making amends, but it had backfired, and tears flowed out of her eyes.

Kay gasped, "Aina, I never meant to bring tears to your eyes."

She pulled out a blue handkerchief with beautiful designs on it and wiped her tears at the speed of light. She did not want to be vulnerable anymore.

"Is that handmade?" Kay asked.

"I made it," Aina said coldly.

"It is incredible indeed. Where did you learn?"

"I went to sewing class with Mother a few times. I found the art intriguing, and I joined as a student last year."

"Last year?" He twitched his eyebrows in surprise. "I... I didn't... I didn't know."

"We told you a few times, but you seemed busy and very

occupied."
Kay looked to the other side, picking the back of his neck.
He sighed softly.

Chapter 6 - Rendezvous with a Stranger

"Where exactly are we going?" He changed the topic.

"It's just a few steps away. It's the barn we bought in June last year, but it has been unoccupied since then. There aren't many people living there, so it was the best place I could think of."

"Smart thinking, maybe you are becoming like me finally," Kay teased. But soon after he had said this statement, he contemplated that it was not a good joke, and definitely not something that could cheer Aina up.

They entered the barn, which looked quite neat for a place that has been unoccupied for one year. Kay said, "Maybe father sends in workers from time to time to clean this area. Good for us."

They cleared some areas and allowed the horse to rest there.

"Neil would be looking for Knight Rider. Yesterday, he told me this horse was the most productive. He said it was like family."

"Family?" Aina smirked.

"Why, what happened?" Kay asked curiously.

"Nothing," she replied.

Just then, they heard the voice of a man calling them out, "Who are you, how did you enter?"

The kids turned around in shock. Kay whispered, "You said this place was unoccupied?"

Aina said, "It should be. That's what I know."

"But who is this man?

The man yelled again, "What are you whispering? This is Mr. Parson's property."

Kay gathered the courage and said, "We are his children."

The man was shocked. With a little recollection exercise, he confirmed that these kids were indeed the Parsons.

"But who are you?" Aina asked.

"Umm... I live in the small hut close to this barn. When I saw you, I quickly ran here. No one has been visiting for the last year, so I thought you were thieves."

Kay questioned, "So you don't work for my father? And you still showed concern for his property. Thank you, Sir. What is your name?"

"Aamed."

"And what do you do?"

"I am a farmer. But I take up other jobs when the cultivation season is gone. I have two kids, just like you. They would love to meet you."

"Sure, we would visit your house someday," Aina said.

"Who else is in your family?"

"Six people in total. My mom, dad, wife, myself, and two kids. My relatives keep visiting too," Aamed replied.

"That's a huge family. I would love to live in a joint family such as yours!" Aina exclaimed.

"Yes, but this life is also full of hardships. My salary is not as big as the family. Sometimes it is difficult to feed everyone," he chuckled, trying to hide the pain.

Aina and Kay were disappointed to hear the depressing news. They led such a lavish lifestyle with everything at their fingertips, while some people struggled to have a proper meal.

Chapter 7 - A Blossoming Friendship

Aamed asked, "If you do not mind, can I touch the horse?"

"Sure," they replied. "His name is Knight Rider."

"That is an awesome name. I owned a horse when I was younger and richer. We were very close. But I had to sell it when we faced financial troubles. Seeing this horse has made my day. Thank you."

Aamed touched Knight Rider's body and caressed him. He seemed joyous. Knight Rider neighed with great energy and enthusiasm. It looked like the heavenly reunion of two long-lost friends, despite the fact that they had met just a few minutes ago.

Aamed then backed off with a shudder. "Anyways, I will leave now. Sorry to have disturbed you."

But Knight Rider did not want him to leave. He bleated, as if complaining, which indicated that he wanted Aamed to stay.

Kay said, "I think he likes you. Maybe you should stay for some time. I am going out with Aina for some time, can you look after it?"

The kind man was happy to do so. It was a blessing for him, as he got to spend more time with Knight Rider without it being awkward.

The kids then went out and inquired in the neighborhood. Indeed, Neil was searching for his horse. He had spread the word amongst the locals that his horse had been stolen from the barn at night and that whoever had news about it would be awarded money and jewels. The locals were eager and excited. They would do anything to find the horse and inform Mr. Devin of its whereabouts.

Aina said, "Our barn is on the outskirts of the town, no one would bother to check there. Also, they wouldn't suspect us since this barn is associated with the family name. So I believe we are safe for now."

Kay responded, "Maybe. But we cannot continue to live like this forever. This horse cannot be found with us. We have to find someone who can take Knight Rider far away from the village. That way, we will not be caught."

"Yes, I know. And I am ready for it. I will feel sad while giving away Knight Rider, but it's the best option."

They returned to the barn and found Knight Rider enjoying himself with Aamed.

"Thank you, Sir," Kay said. "You have been very helpful and cooperative."

Aamed then made an exit, while the kids bid him farewell.

Aina then had an idea. "Come on, Knight Rider! Let's go out and have some fun!" She started accompanying him outside the barn, but Kay had an objection. "Did we just discuss that we cannot be seen with him at any cost?"

"Yes, we did talk about that a few minutes ago."

"Then, what changed now?"

"He needs to run and breathe in the fresh air. Only for a few minutes, please join us. He hasn't run on an open field for months now," Aina said.

"How do you know that?"

"Umm... It's my assumption, looking at his dismal condition. What matters is we have to make him happy."

Outside, there were stretches of fresh green grass as far as the eyes could see. It was a refreshing scene to watch. Knight Rider happily played around in the large space. It trotted around and neighed. It seemed pleased to be there. Suddenly, Aina climbed onto its back. Kay screamed, "What are you doing, get down!"

"I am sorry, but I can't obey your command today, only for today!"

Chapter 8 - Horse Riding

"Don't be silly, you might get hurt, come down!" Kay said with his trembling lips.

"Maybe you should come up. Let's ride Knight Rider together! That way, you can protect me, and I can have fun too."

"That is not happening. You know I can't touch him, he could have germs on his body! I will protect you by getting you down," Kay said. He reached for Aina's body to pick her up, but Aina quickly grabbed his arm and said, "Today is our first and last day with it." She placed his hand on Knight Rider's soft mane. Kay felt delirious by the touch. This was the first time he had touched a horse or an animal. Kay felt the horse, its every breath, and movement.

Aina finally said, hoping that this would convince Kay, "You very well know that you haven't enjoyed life even a little bit. You always do things for father, for business, for me... I know. Today, for one more time, do this for me. For your little sister. Get on Knight Rider, and let's embark on this mini-adventure together!"

Kay hesitantly agreed, only because he couldn't let Aina take the risk on her own. He too, with great difficulty, mounted upon the horse, and the both of them set out for an adventure - Horse Riding! Kay was terrified at first, he kept thinking that they were going to hit the ground. But Aina was relishing the ride from the very first moment onwards.

"Where did you learn horse riding?" Kay screamed. His shoulders were tight from the fear and his eyes blinked rapidly.

"I am not as boring as you are! I have many other talents as well," Aina replied, her hair flying hither and thither with the wind.

Both of them laughed and Kay soon forgot about all the frightening thoughts in his mind. He now had complete trust and control over Knight Rider. They rode for miles, under the open blue sky, in the fresh air, on the lush green grass. Everything seemed so heavenly with Knight Rider.

Kay had had fun days in his life, but those were limited to his definition of fun, that is, maybe a visit to a book fair, a felicitation ceremony, or a good board meeting. He had never had this sort of fun. That day was undoubtedly the best day of his life. He had touched a horse (who could have had germs on it) and ridden it with his sister. It was a huge milestone.

"Aina!" He cried.

"Yes!" She replied.

"I am sorry!" He said.

"For what?" Aina questioned doubtfully.

"I am sorry for saying what I said."

Aina's joyous mood turned into an emotional one. Knight Rider stopped and they got off.

Kay said, "Aina, it's not your fault. Whatever I said in the morning, I was just frustrated. Very frustrated. I know I made you feel like a burden, but it's not true. And I am so sorry."

"I did steal, and I deserved some scolding too," Aina said.

"And... I have been spending more time at the office. I

haven't been talking to you as well. I will try to divide my time between the office and Neil, and you."

"It's okay, I guess. I may not like Neil, but I like that he supports you," Aina stated.

Chapter 9 - The Parson Duo in the Soup

The next morning, when they woke up, what was feared had happened. The villagers had informed Mr. Devin that his horse was in the Parson family's barn. He was down in the living room to talk with Mr. Parson.

As the kids got dressed and entered the living room, their worry and tension intensified.

Mr. Devin said, "One of my well-wishers notified me that my horse was seen in your barn yesterday afternoon. That barn in the outskirts registered under your name - I wanted to talk about that."

Mr. Parson said, "There is a mistake, I believe. We would never engage in such a thing."

"Yes, I trust you. But the villagers..."

"What did they say?"

"One of them says he saw Aina and Kay riding my horse."

Aina and Kay exchanged horrified glances.

Mr. Parson chuckled, "They are making up these stories to acquire the reward you have announced. None of this is real; my kids can never do that."

Aina whispered to Kay, "He did not even question us."

Kay replied, "That is because he trusts us. And we might have broken that trust by stealing Knight Rider."

Mr. Parson added, "You know how well-mannered Kay is, and Neil and Kay are such good friends."

"Yes, Kay is indeed a gem. And Aina... Umm... She is also very sweet. But we should confirm once, to silence the villagers once and for all," Mr. Devin said.

"I don't think you should doubt us, and we need not prove ourselves. But for your satisfaction, let us visit the place once," Mr. Parson agreed.

"Thank you so much," Mr. Devin said with a wide phony grin.

Aina and Kay were petrified. What would they do now? Kay's elbows pressed against his body. He had frozen for a while. After a few moments, he said in a shaky voice, "Aina, Knight Rider is sleeping there peacefully. I cannot even begin to imagine what would happen if they found him there."

"We will be chastised. I can take that for him," Aina replied innocently.

"That is not the end of it. People will defame us in front of the entire village. We are the Parson family - the most civilized, classiest, and the most royal of all. The villagers would create and spread all sorts of rumors if they got to know about this."

They walked hurriedly out of the house. Mr. Devin and Mr. Parson sat in the car, heading to the barn. Aina knew the shorter route, so they took that route, determined to reach the place earlier than the elders and then think of a solution.

They ran and ran and ran. Kay was still thinking about their reputation bursting into flames. Aina wondered what would happen to Knight Rider. "Would we have to give Knight Rider back to him?" Aina asked.

"That is what you are pondering on? We have to return it. And then apologize. And then make a good excuse to curb the damage."

"We cannot give it back to him. I don't think he can treat

him well," Aina showed concern.

"Let's reach there first. We will see what situation arises and how to manage it. As of now, think of reasonable excuses."

Chapter 10 - Confrontation

They reached the barn and scanned it with their eyes. There was no one around except the stolen horse. Mr. Devin and Mr. Parson had not yet arrived. It was a golden opportunity for them to escape with Knight Rider. They thought they could take him out for a while, and then the elders would leave when they found the barn empty. No one will be caught, and it would be a happy ending. They could see what was to be done with Knight Rider later.

But not all things in life are as easy as ABC, and not all plans work as smoothly as thought to be. The Parson Duo's plan also did not work out as thought. When they were leading Knight Rider outside the barn, Mr. Devin and Mr. Parson arrived and caught them red-handed. To add insult to injury, Neil arrived on the spot and gazed with perplexity in his mind.

Mr. Parson took a step back. His eyes widened. His heartbeat fastened. He did not move or utter a word for a few moments. Aina and Kay had tears in their eyes. They could not even imagine how he felt when he saw them with the horse. Maybe he doubted that all the values he had imparted had vanished; or that he wasn't successful as a father. They knew that this was a painful moment.

Everyone could hear Aina's quick, deep breaths. She said, "We can explain."

"You stole the horse?" Mr. Parson asked in utter disbelief. The kids were silent. Their silence proved everything.

Aina started, "I am sorry. I had to. Maybe this was the wrong way but-"

"Yes, this was the wrong way! I don't understand. Why did you have to do this? And Kay, you were with her in this? You are elder and smarter. I did not expect this from both of you!"

The kids' heads hung in shame. Kay said, "Aina told me about it. I am sure she has a reason behind this."

"What reason? Reason for robbery? Don't we give you enough at home?"

Aina remained quiet. Kay signaled her to speak something, to tell their father the reason behind her committing this crime.

"If you had ever asked for a horse, I would have got you a hundred beautiful ones. Why did you have to steal? Mr. Devin, I am extremely sorry for the inconvenience caused. I apologize on behalf of my kids. I will ensure that they face the consequences. I assure you nothing like this will happen in the future."

Mr. Devin said, "It's okay, they are only kids. But I didn't expect this kind of behavior from Kay. I thought he was quite mature and intelligent for his age. Anyways, let bygones be bygones."

Neil finally broke his silence. "You are a thief, Kay!"

"I am sorry!" Kay said.

"How can I be sure you won't commit the same fraud in business too? How can I trust you now?"

Aina stared at Mr. Devin and Neil furiously.

"You can trust him; it is not his fault. I stole the horse, and he just fulfilled his role as a brother," Aina said, trying to convince Neil.

"You're lying again, aren't you? Father, I don't think Kay

can be my partner anymore!"

Mr. Devin said, "We will talk about it later." It was evident he was trying to handle the situation.

Neil and his servants tried to bring the horse along but failed to do so. Knight Rider screamed in agony. He clearly did not want to go.

Aina said, "He won't come. He wants to stay with us."

Mr. Parson rebuked, "Aina, quiet!"

Knight Rider then kicked Neil, and he fell to the ground. The poor horse ran towards Aina and Kay. Everyone was bewildered. How could the horse be so affectionate with Aina and Kay, but at the same time, kick its real owner?

Chapter 11 - Why did Aina Steal

There was another failed attempt to take Knight Rider back to its original place. Mr. Parson and Kay had no clue of what was happening.

Aina had to explain. "When we visited Mr. Devin's stable, I understood that the horse's condition is not normal. It looked very different from the horses in our stable. They are all fit, young and healthy. But look at this horse, Father; he is so thin, weak, and malnourished!"

Mr. Parson agreed to what his daughter was saying. But he did not speak a word. He helped Neil get up from the ground. Kay had too noticed the horse's poor situation.

"Then, I decided to dig deeper. I found out that Neil does not feed his horses and other animals properly and makes them work all day long!"

Mr. Parson was dumbfounded. Kay's mind flashed back to all the times they had discussed this, but he had not been able to decipher Aina's helplessness.

Mr. Parson said, "This is a very serious allegation. Do you have any proof?"

"Yes, I have heard his servants speaking about it. The behavioral pattern and physical appearance of Knight Rider, I mean, the horse, makes it evident."

Mr. Devin said, "She is just making baseless arguments! Why should we believe a notorious kid anyway?"

Aina added, "There is more to the story. That night, I saw Neil hurting Knight Rider!"

"What?" Kay exclaimed in shock. "Is that why you brought Knight Rider along with you that night?"

"Yes. I did not want him to face any more torture there," Aina said with tears in her eyes.

Mr. Parson said, "Animal abuse is a crime, Mr. Devin. I believe the required investigation should be done. If this is true, you should be punished for it."

Kay said, "Animals are one of the most essential beings for human survival and the purest souls. Cruelty towards them is one of the most heinous crimes. You should be ashamed of what you have done. I admired you and saw you as an inspiration, but if this is true, I consider you no less than a criminal."

Aina added, "Knight Rider is such a loyal, biddable and obedient pet, and you did not treat him well. He did not deserve to be treated like this. He deserves to be treated with love."

Kay, Aina, and Mr. Parson drove home and had some rest, for everyone was exhausted. In the evening, they sat together and had an emotional reunion.

Kay finally said, "I am sorry! I could not understand your turmoil. How stupid I was!"

"Well, the word stupid does not suit you," Aina smiled.

"I never understood how my little sister grew up so fast. But why didn't you tell me about this? I had asked you several times."

Aina replied, "Neil is your best friend and your business partner. You have been with him for several years. Mr. Devin is like your mentor and guide. You look up to him. They are the two people you like the most. I didn't think you would believe me."

Kay said, "You had to go through such an internal tumult,

all alone. Yes, you are correct. But you got two things absolutely wrong. First, all of this was in the past. My ideologies have changed, for the better. So you must start using past tense now."

"And what is the second thing?"

"At any point in my entire life, there has been only one person I have loved the most. It's you, Aina!"

"The feeling is mutual," Aina replied, feeling elated.

"I may not be able to express it, or spend time with you, but I truly love you. And there is nothing that can change that."

"But your business, everything's gone now! It's a big loss, all because of me."

Chapter 12 - The New Owner

"That is not your share of troubles. What you did was the right thing. But you should have informed us. We are family, and we will always believe you over outsiders."

Later that day, the case was reported to the police for investigation. Knight Rider was with the Parson family. Mr. Parson said, "Mr. Devin does not deserve to have Knight Rider back. So let us keep him with us. He has also settled well with you, Aina and Kay."

Aina said, "No, father. We should not keep it with us. I know someone who can take better care of him than we can."

Kay was perplexed. "After all this time, you want to give it away? You have fought for it. It's yours!"

"I want to be with Knight Rider, but there is a person who needs him."

"Who are you talking about?" Mr. Parson asked. Maybe Kay already knew the answer.

Aina revealed, "Aamed."

"And, who is he?" Mr. Parson questioned curiously, for he wanted to know who this person was for whom his daughter was ready to abandon Knight Rider.

"Father, he is a poor farmer. He lives near that barn. He is struggling to feed his family of six. He had to sell off his horse to supplement his income. I believe we should gift him this horse."

"But do you think he can take care of him?" Mr. Parson

asked. He was doubtful about giving off Knight Rider to a stranger.

Kay assured his father, "We have met him, and he seems to be very industrious and kind-hearted."

Mr. Parson said, "Knight Rider has just been out of an abusive household. We cannot just send him anywhere. And besides, if the farmer is so poor, how will he take care of a horse? Does he even want it?"

Aina and Kay thought that their father had a valid point. Simply giving away the horse would neither help Aamed nor Knight Rider. They had to think of something else.

An idea struck Kay's genius mind. "Aina, remember when we visited the stable down the house?"

"Yes! I do. It was very crowded," Aina answered. She got the hang of what Kay was proposing.

"So, I think we should consider shifting some of our animals to that barn and make it operational," Kay suggested.

Mr. Parson was elated, "That is awesome thinking, kids. Let's do this. But how is it related to what we were discussing, about Knight Rider and the farmer?"

"Knight Rider can stay more comfortably at that barn. So, we will transport him there. And then, we could appoint Aamed as the attendant-in-charge!"

"But do you think he is good enough for the job?"

Aina said, "He cares about the barn, about your property. He also has a way with animals. He gets along well with Knight Rider.

Kay added, "He is a local, and that can be very beneficial. You can talk to him once. Appoint him to the post if you like him."

"I will surely keep that in mind. Both of you are so mature

and sensible now. I am proud of you," Mr. Parson said.

"We have learned it from you!" They said.

A month later, Kay and Aina's suggestion was adopted, and Aamed was appointed the Chief Attendant of the barn. It was a massive indicator that good things happen to good people, and bad people are punished for their deeds.

If one had to choose, among all siblings, the most conflicted-yet-loving pair would be Kay and Aina.

www.ingramcontent.com/pod-product-compliance
Lightning Source LLC
La Vergne TN
LVHW050423160726

843469LV00041B/1204